Tina's Taxi

Written by Betsy Franco
Pictures by Mercedes McDonald

TIPTON ELEMENTARY PRIMARY

SCHOLASTIC INC.

New York   Toronto   London   Auckland   Sydney

Copyright © 1994 by Scholastic Inc.
All rights reserved. Published by Scholastic Inc.
Printed in the U.S.A.
ISBN 0-590-27536-4

20 19 18 17 16 15   08   00

Tina drives a taxi.

She calls it Old Yellow.

She washes her taxi until it shines.

On Monday, she picks up Meg.

On Tuesday, she picks up Tim.

On Wednesday, she picks up Will.

On Thursday, she picks up Ted.

On Friday, she picks up Fran.

On Saturday, she picks up Sam.

On Sunday, she always takes the day off.

She washes her taxi until it shines.

And then Tina goes to visit her friends.
Guess what she does?

She rides her bicycle!